HELLO, I'M THEA!

I'm *Geronimo Stilton*. As I'm sure you know from my bestselling novels, I'm a special correspondent for *The Rodent's Gazette*, Mouse Island's most famous newspaper. Unlike my 'fraidy mouse brother, I adore traveling, having adventures, and meeting rodents from all around the world!

The adventure I want to tell you about begins at Mouseford Academy, the school I went to when I was a young mouseling. I had such a great experience there as a student that I came back to teach a journalism class.

When I returned as a grown mouse, I met five really special students: Colette, Nicky, Pamela, Paulina, and Violet. You could hardly imagine five more different mouselings, but they became great friends right away. And they liked me so much that they decided to name their group after me: the Thea Sisters! I was so touched by that, I decided to write about their adventures. So turn the page to read a fabumouse adventure about the

THEA SISTERS!

Name: Nicky
Nickname: Nic
Home: Australia
Secret ambition: Wants to be an ecologist.
Loves: Open spaces and nature.
Strengths: She is always in a good mood, as long as she's outdoors!
Weaknesses: She can't sit still!
Secret: Nicky is claustrophobic — she can't stand being in small, tight places.

Nicky

COLETTE

Name: Colette

Nickname: It's Colette, please. (She can't stand nicknames.)

Home: France

Secret ambition: Colette is very particular about her appearance. She wants to be a fashion writer.

Loves: The color pink.

Strengths: She's energetic and full of great ideas.

Weaknesses: She's always late!

Secret: To relax, there's nothing Colette likes more than a manicure and pedicure.

Colette

Name: Violet
Nickname: Vi
Home: China

VIOLET

Secret ambition: Wants to become a great violinist.

Loves: Books! She is a real intellectual, just like my brother, Geronimo.

Strengths: She's detail-oriented and always open to new things.

Weaknesses: She is a bit sensitive and can't stand being teased. And if she doesn't get enough sleep, she can be a real grouch!

Secret: She likes to unwind by listening to classical music and drinking green tea.

Violet

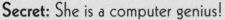

Name: Paulina
Nickname: Polly
Home: Peru
Secret ambition: Wants to be a scientist.
Loves: Traveling and meeting people from all over the world. She is also very close to her sister, Maria.
Strengths: Loves helping other rodents.
Weaknesses: She's shy and can be a bit clumsy.
Secret: She is a computer genius!

PAULINA

Name: Pamela
Nickname: Pam
Home: Tanzania

PAMELA

Secret ambition: Wants to become a sports journalist or a car mechanic.

Loves: Pizza, pizza, and more pizza! She'd eat pizza for breakfast if she could.

Strengths: She is a peacemaker. She can't stand arguments.

Weaknesses: She is very impulsive.

Secret: Give her a screwdriver and any mechanical problem will be solved!

Pamela

Geronimo Stilton

Thea Stilton
AND THE
SECRET CITY

Scholastic Inc.

New York   Toronto   London   Auckland

Sydney   Mexico City   New Delhi   Hong Kong

ISBN 978-0-545-15061-3

Based on an original idea by Elisabetta Dami.

www.geronimostilton.com

Published by Scholastic Inc., 557 Broadway, New York, NY 10012. SCHOLASTIC and associated logos are trademarks and/or registered trademarks of Scholastic Inc.

Stilton is the name of a famous English cheese. It is a registered trademark of the Stilton Cheese Makers' Association. For more information, go to www.stiltoncheese.com.

Text by Thea Stilton
Original title *La città segreta*
Cover by Red Whale
Illustrations by Alessandro Battan, Fabio Bono, Sergio Cabella, Barbara Di Muzio, Paolo Ferrante, Marco Meloni, Manuela Razzi, Arianna Rea, Fabio Bonechi, Ketty Formaggio, Daniela Geremia, Donatella Melchionno, and Micaela Tangorra
Graphics by Laura Zuccotti and Paola Cantoni

Special thanks to Beth Dunfey
Translated by Julia Heim
Interior design by Kay Petronio

12 11 10 9 8   12 13 14 15 16/0

Printed in the U.S.A.   40
First printing, June 2010

A MESSAGE
CUT SHORT

I had just come back from a **FABUMOUSE** vacation to Mouse Island's **NATURE RESERVE PARK**. I'd spent three days hiking all the way to the Lake Lake. The trip was **INTENSE, FILLED WITH ADVENTURE, AND THOROUGHLY EXHAUSTING.**

MOUSE ISLAND'S NATURE RESERVE PARK

In other words, it was my favorite kind of vacation!

When I got home to my mouse hole, I was beat! I dumped my backpack by the door, **SLOUCHED** to the living room, and sprawled on the couch.

Oh, dear me, I almost forgot to introduce myself. My name is Stilton, Thea Stilton. I am a special correspondent for *The Rodent's Gazette,* the most famouse newspaper on Mouse Island. Usually, I love nothing more than to be on the open road, feeling the wind in my fur. But just this once, I was really happy to be home.

I closed my eyes for a moment. When I opened them, I saw the light on my answering machine BLINKING. I gathered the little strength I had left and pressed PLAY. As a journalist, I have to stay in touch with my contacts, and it doesn't pay to fall behind on my squeakmail.

FIRST MESSAGE: "Hi, Thea! I wanted to ask you about your catamaran . . . Oh, I forgot you were on vacation!" **CLICK!**

The squeak belonged to my friend **Penelope Poisonfur**. We'd met during a survival course.

SECOND MESSAGE: "Thea, it's me, Penelope! Do you remember the Alpine guide who . . . Oh, for the love of cheese, are you still away?" **CLICK!**

THIRD MESSAGE: "Hello, Thea? I was calling to find out if—Oh, right, you're still on that trip!" **CLICK!**

The fourth, fifth, and sixth messages were also

Penelope: "All right already, Thea! Are you ever planning to come home?" **CLICK!**

When I heard the seventh message, I **jumped** up from the couch: "Hi, Thea. It's PAULINA. I'm in Cuzco. I need a—" **CLICK!**

Crispy **cheese fritters**! The answering machine had run out of memory! Paulina's message had been cut off.

What was Paulina doing in Cuzco, PERU? Why wasn't she with the other

Pamela PAULINA Colette Violet Nicky

My friends, the Thea Sisters!

THEA SISTERS at MOUSEFORD ACADEMY on Whale Island?

Despite my exhaustion, my paws were itching to find out!

Oh! I'm so **tired**, I haven't explained who the THEA SISTERS are yet. I'm *fonder* of those five mouselings than I am of my own fur. I first met Colette, *Nicky*, Pamela, PAULINA, and **Violet** at MOUSEFORD ACADEMY when I was teaching a course on ADVENTURE journalism. It was almost as if I'd adopted them. I feel like their big sister.

My eyes moved toward my laptop, which was sitting on my desk. Suddenly, a thought occurred to me!

Of course! Paulina never went anywhere without her laptop! I hurried over and checked my E-MAIL.

My hunch was right! Paulina had sent me

a **looong** e-mail. It was the latest installment in the adventures of the THEA SISTERS.

This time, my five dear mouselings were in South America, in faraway PERU! The e-mail was accompanied by beautiful digital photos. And that's not all! The music of the Andes played from my computer.

HOW AMAZING! I felt like I was there in Peru with five of my *favorite* rodents by my side.

As soon as I finished reading Paulina's note, I knew I had the subject of my next book: THE SECRET CITY!

It all started on Whale Island one warm spring morning. . . .

HERE'S HOW IT ALL BEGAN . . .

The **SUN** was high in the sky and blazing brightly. It was hotter than a freshly grilled **cheese sandwich**! On Whale Island, it was hard to find more than a square inch of **SHADE**. The Thea Sisters had been hanging out in HAWK WOODS for hours. Violet, Paulina, and Colette were perched on a **ROCK**, armed with a video camera and **binoculars**, while Nicky and Pamela were sitting on the branch of an old OAK tree. Nicky had her camera ready, and Pamela was holding a powerful microphone capable of capturing even the faintest **CHIRP**.

The object of their attention was a **small** hole on the face of **Mount Landslide**.

A couple of hawks had built a nest there. The five mouselings wanted to capture the moment when the eggs hatched. If they could get the scoop for the school blog, it'd be bigger than a sighting of the Lochmouse Monster! They'd be sure to get the **best** grade in their writing class. It isn't easy to get close to a hawk's NEST!

Violet signaled her friends with one paw. Something was **MOVING** in the nest.

THE TIME HAD COME AT LAST!

Right at that moment . . . RIIINNNGG!!!

Paulina's cell phone began ringing. Paulina

was so surprised, she nearly slipped off the edge of the cliff.

A shrill screech came from the hole in the rock.

SCREEEEEEEEEEEEEEEEEE!

The mother hawk had noticed them. And she was ANGRIER than a cat with a BAD case of fleas!

There went the Thea Sisters' scoop!

There was only one thing to do: Scamper off as fast as their paws could take them!

However, Violet soon realized that someone was missing! Paulina was still talking on her phone.

Violet scurried BACK and dragged her away. "Does this seem like the right moment to be chattering?" she asked. "If that falcon catches us, we're catnip!" But she soon regretted the way she'd squeaked when she saw that her friend's big BLACK EYES were filled with tears.

MORE THAN FRIENDS!

As soon as the mouselings got back to MOUSEFORD ACADEMY, Paulina headed straight to the headmaster's office. She was with *Professor Octavius de Mousus* for a full half hour.

Colette, Nicky, Pamela, and Violet waited for her outside the office door. They were worried about Paulina. As the minutes ticked by, they seemed to stretch longer and longer. Pamela, in particular, was growing *IMPATIENT*.

"What could be taking

so long?" she cried. "I could've changed a flat tire while BLINDFOLDED in the time she's been in there!"

Nicky put a paw on her friend's shoulder. "I'm sure she'll be out in a minute, Pam."

Pam nodded. "I just **hope** everything's okay."

At that moment, Paulina emerged from the office. Her *friends* immediately gathered around her.

"Paulina, if you have a problem . . . if you need help . . ." Colette began.

"We need to know what's wrong!" exclaimed Pamela. "You're turning us into a bunch of **worryrats** here!"

"We're more than friends! We're sisters!" Nicky burst out. "Tell us what's going on."

"Of course she will!" said Violet. "There aren't any secrets among the THEA

SISTERS, and there never will be!"

Paulina was **moved** by her friends' concern. "You're right," she said as she led them back to the dormitory. "I will tell you everything while I pack my bags!"

More than friends—sisters!

"**YOU'RE LEAVING?!**" her friends shouted in unison as they scurried after her.

"Yes. I need to get back to Peru as soon as possible!" explained Paulina. She opened the door to their room. "That phone call was from my sister, Maria. One of our dear friends is in more **tRouble** than a mouse at the annual cat convention!"

"No need for explanations!" Nicky said, cutting her off. "You'll tell us during the trip. You didn't think we'd let you go by yourself, did you?"

"You mean you'll come to **Peru** with me?" exclaimed Paulina. "You're the best friends a mouse could ask for! THANK YOU!"

Before she'd finished squeaking, her friends had started packing their bags.

SOUTH AMERICA

The name *America* comes from the name of the Italian navigator Amerigo Vespucci (1454–1512), one of the first Europeans to explore the coast of South America.

THE NUMBERS

The Andes make up the longest chain of high mountains in the world. They extend for more than 5,000 miles and over seven countries: Venezuela, Colombia, Ecuador, Peru, Bolivia, Chile, and Argentina. Many peaks are more than 20,000 feet high. Only the Himalayas are higher.

Lake Titicaca, the highest navigable lake in the world, is 12,500 feet above sea level. It is located on the border between Bolivia and Peru and was a sacred place for the Incas.

VENEZUELA
TRINIDAD
GUYANA
SURINAME
COLOMBIA
FRENCH GUIANA
ECUADOR
BRAZIL
PERU
BOLIVIA
PARAGUAY
CHILE
URUGUAY
ARGENTINA

A SPECIAL RODENT

After taking a boat to Mouse Island, the mouselings boarded a plane to Peru. Once Colette, Nicky, Pamela, PAULINA, and **Violet** had settled in for the flight, Paulina started to tell her story.

"Like I told you, I got a call from my sister, Maria," Paulina began. "It's PROFESSOR SAGEFUR. His son got lost, so he left by himself, but he's in danger!"

"Whoa, whoa, whoa! Hold on a second," said Pamela. "Start from the beginning. I haven't understood a single SQUEAK!"

"First, tell us who this professor is," suggested Violet.

Paulina pulled out a PHOTO of her sister, Maria, when she was just a tiny mouseling. She was sitting on the lap of an older rodent

PROFESSOR SAGEFUR

MARIA

wearing a Santa Mouse costume. "The mouse in the picture is **PROFESSOR SAGEFUR**."

"Who?! Santa Mouse?" asked Colette.

"Yes, the one dressed as Santa Mouse. This was a very **SAD** Christmas for Maria and me. It was the first after our parents disappeared. Our aunt and uncle were taking

care of us, and they tried everything they could to cheer us up, but no one could get little Maria to crack a SMILE.

"Then PROFESSOR SAGEFUR came along. He was an old friend of my mom and dad's. He dressed up in a Santa Mouse costume and he even got a carriage covered with little bells and drove us all over the city. As soon as

she saw him in that costume, Maria started to SMILE!"

"What an **incredible** rodent!" commented Pamela.

"Yes, he's really special. Maria is very close to him. When she called me, I just knew I had to get home and help her find him."

"So what happened to the professor?" asked Nicky.

"The professor and his son, GONZALO, are famous **ARCHAEOLOGISTS**," explained Paulina. "While GONZALO was away on an expedition, he **DISAPPEARED**. For days and days, the professor waited, but he didn't hear any news from his son. So, finally, he left to go and look for him in the ANDES, even though it's the rainy season! And now it's been days

Gonzalo

since Maria's heard from him. She's sick with *worry*."

"Don't **WORRY**, Paulina!" Violet said reassuringly. "We're here to help you. We'll find PROFESSOR SAGEFUR *FASTER* than you can say 'goat cheese Gorgonzola with pepper jack on top,' and we'll help him find **GONZALO**, too!"

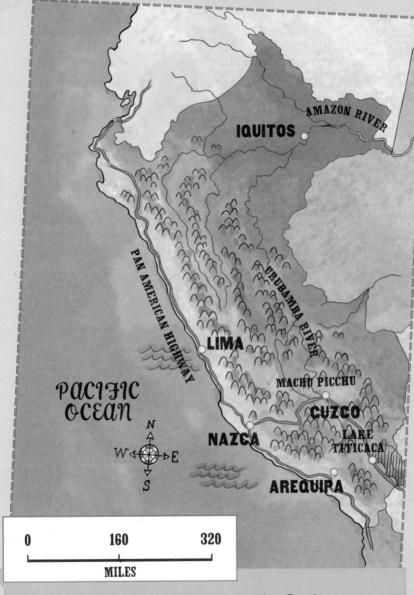

AMAZON RIVER

IQUITOS

PAN AMERICAN HIGHWAY

URUBAMBA RIVER

LIMA

PACIFIC OCEAN

N
W   E
S

MACHU PICCHU

CUZCO

LAKE TITICACA

NAZCA

AREQUIPA

| 0 | 160 | 320 |
MILES

Every map is drawn to a certain scale. On this map,
1 inch corresponds to 160 miles.

PERU!

Capital: Lima

Land mass: 496,225 square miles

Population: around 29 million

Official languages: Spanish and Quechua

Other languages: Aymara, Campa, and Aguaruna

Money: Nuevo sol

The first inhabitants of Peru were hunters and gatherers who lived in caves along the coast. The oldest site, Pikimachay, dates from 12,000 B.C. Cotton, beans, squash, and chili peppers were planted around 4000 B.C. Later, the Chavin culture introduced weaving and religion before disappearing around 300 B.C. Over the centuries, many other cultures, like the Nazca, prospered in different regions of the country.

The Incas absorbed traditions from many previous cultures to form a single culture that covered an immense territory. This was possible thanks to the roads that they built, which allowed for communication between far-flung, remote areas that were previously inaccessible.

By the early fifteenth century, the Incas dominated Peru and parts of modern-day Chile, Ecuador, Bolivia, and Colombia. Then, between 1526 and 1528, the first of the Spanish conquistadors arrived to explore Peru's coastal regions.

The Spaniards conquered the Incas and made Peru a Spanish colony in 1532. Peru finally won its independence from Spain in 1824. Today it is a democratic republic.

LITTLE SISTER

After a long day and night of traveling, the Thea Sisters touched ground in the city of Cuzco.

"Wipe the sleep off your whiskers, mouselings!" exclaimed Colette. "Have you ever seen such a fabumouse sight?"

"Fabumouse is right!" agreed Violet, peering out of the plane window. Before them was a graceful city nestled among mountain peaks. The **R E D** roofs of the houses glittered in the morning sunlight.

After they scrambled off the plane, the mouselings found Maria and Paulina's aunt and uncle waiting for them.

"Big Sister!" they heard someone yell. Maria was so excited, she was jumping up and down like a kangaroo. She **threw her**

paws around Paulina, almost knocking her big sister down.

Paulina exclaimed, "By all that's cheesy and delicious, I can't even hold you up anymore! How much have you GROWN in these last few months?"

"Almost two inches!" answered Maria. Her eyes were gleaming with happiness. It was obvious that she had missed her sister.

Paulina introduced her friends to Maria one by one. It was friendship at first squeak between the little one and the Thea Sisters!

After they finished hugging and shaking paws, the group left the airport.

Luckily, Uncle Pedro and Aunt Nidia had brought their pickup truck. All EIGHT of them and their luggage (including the FOUR HUGE PINK SUITCASES Colette had brought!) fit easily.

CUZCO!

Population: Around 300,000

Elevation: 11,217 feet above sea level

Cuzco was the capital of the Incan empire until the arrival of the Spanish conquistadors in 1533. Francisco Pizarro moved the capital to Lima. Cuzco was home to the famous Temple of the Sun; after the Spanish arrived, much of the structure was torn down and reassembled as a church. It eventually became known as the Cathedral of Santo Domingo.

Cuzco is the oldest inhabited city in the Americas. Today, its winding cobbled streets transport visitors back in time to Incan ruins and temples, colonial churches, and mansions.

THE CATHEDRAL OF
SANTO DOMINGO

COMPUTERS AND CELL PHONES

After an hour's drive, they arrived at Uncle Pedro and Aunt Nidia's cozy mouse hole. Paulina immediately got out her LAPTOP.

Before leaving MOUSEFORD ACADEMY, Paulina had been exchanging e-mails with the GREEN MICE. They were an environmental organization with offices all over the world. The members of the group helped one another out by providing information and assistance. Thanks to the Peruvian members of the GREEN MICE, the mouselings had obtained detailed MAPS of the area PROFESSOR SAGEFUR was traveling through.

As Paulina checked on every detail of their EXPEDITION, Maria curled up next to her. She wanted to keep her sister within paw's reach.

"Can I come with you?" she pleaded. "I'll be your assistant! I'll take notes faster than a puma. And I'll carry more mozzarella snacks on my back than any llama in Peru!"

"It's too dangerous!" Aunt Nidia cried before Paulina could squeak. "The ANDES are filled with difficult climbs and POISONOUS creatures! They're no place for a little mouseling!" She ruffled Maria's fur lovingly.

Maria's disappointment was written all over her snout. Paulina put her paw around her sister, then pointed at her laptop. "Don't worry, Maria. I have a **very important** assignment for you."

Maria looked up at her sister eagerly.

"With this computer, you can follow our path," explained Paulina. "You'll monitor our movements closely and contact us right away if we're headed in the **wrong** direction."

"Wait, are you saying this thing can see you all the way up there in the Andes?" **Uncle Pedro** asked in disbelief.

Paulina smiled. "Maria won't see me in the fur and Bone . . . but she will be able to see the **SATELLITE** signal from my **CELL PHONE**!" She turned back to her little sister. "This way, you'll never lose sight of our position, and you'll always know just where we are."

Uncle Pedro threw up his paws. "Computers! Cell phones! I'm just an old-fashioned rodent. I don't understand how it all works, *but I trust you*. If you tell me that this will help keep you safe, then I believe you."

Violet had another special job for Maria. "I can't bring Frilly with me," she began. Frilly was her pet cricket. "I hate to be separated from him, but I'm afraid he won't be able to stand the COLD of the mountains. Would you be willing to take care of him for me?"

Maria's eyes lit up when she saw Frilly's tiny head pop out of his pumpkin home. "Of course I will, Violet! You can trust me! I'll be the best cricket-sitter in the world, you'll see!"

CHIRP! CHIRP!

THE ROAD TO MACHU PICCHU

Two hours before **SUNRISE** the next morning, the *Thea Sisters* set out on their journey. The mouselings were sleepier than a hibernating badger. Paulina was the only one who was completely awake. She sat next to her uncle, who was in the driver's seat. He would take them to the train bound for **MACHU PICCHU**.

Paulina was glad for the opportunity to ask him about Maria.

"Your sister is doing quite well!" her uncle assured her. "She misses you, that's only natural, but she is also very, very proud of you! She talks about MOUSEFORD ACADEMY as if she were there with you. She's always squeaking to her friends that one day she will go there and become a *Thea Sister* herself!"

Paulina was **glad** to hear Maria was doing so well. It was hard for her to be so far away from her beloved little sister.

Meanwhile, outside the windows, the streets of CUZCO glowed in the light of the streetlamps. "This place is so beautiful.

It reminds me a little of home," Colette murmured, thinking wistfully of PARIS.

When they reached the station, Paulina hugged her uncle. Then she and her friends scampered on board the train.

After nearly four hours, they arrived at Aguas Calientes. Paulina hurried to the car rental desk and rented an ALL-TERRAIN vehicle.

The mouselings' next stop: MACHU PICCHU!

As Pam drove carefully along the twisting roads, Nicky, Colette, and Violet kept calling out in amazement.

"Look, the mountains are covered in **SNOW**!"

"There's a **LLAMA**!"

"And a herd of goats!"

When they reached a certain height, they were struck squeakless. In front of them lay the ruins of **MACHU PICCHU**, the lost city of the Incas. The city was perched below a rocky peak. The streets were laid out in a grid pattern that seemed to cling to the side of a grassy slope. The **STONE WALLS** of its buildings looked ancient. It was an impressive sight.

"Thundering cat tails, it's **AMAZING**!" breathed Pamela.

MACHU PICCHU

Machu Picchu is one of the most important archaeological sites in the world. It is situated 6,562 feet above sea level, on the eastern slope of the Cordillera Vilcanota in the Urubamba River Valley. In the Quechua language, *Machu Picchu* means "ancient peak."

Machu Picchu was built by the Incas, perhaps as a ceremonial center, a royal retreat, or a country palace, in the fifteenth century. The Incas abandoned the city probably around the time of the conquistadors, and its existence remained unknown to the wider world for four hundred years. It is not mentioned in any of the chronicles of the Spanish conquistadors.

Machu Picchu was rediscovered on July 11, 1911, by Hiram Bingham, a professor at Yale University. Bingham wrote a number of books about Machu Picchu, the most famous being *Lost City of the Incas*.

Today, Machu Picchu remains an archaeological site shrouded in mystery. Its buildings and landscape beckon visitors from around the world.

CLOUDS AND CONDORS

Paulina wished she could let her friends relax and enjoy the *fantastic view* of MACHU PICCHU. But she was desperate to carry out their mission: finding Professor Sagefur.

So the mouselings left the URUBAMBA RIVER VALLEY for the vast Andean plateau, where many of the descendants of the Incas still live. Dark clouds covered the sun and a frigid WIND swept through the area. The five friends followed a bare and uneven road without encountering another rodent.

"Are you sure anyone lives **UP HERE**?" Nicky asked Paulina.

"If they do, they're probably smart enough to be inside, away from the **COLD**," commented Violet. "I'm freezing my **tail** off!"

"**THERE! DOWN THERE!**" Colette interrupted, pointing out her window. "Those are **LLAMAS**, right?! There's even a shepherd!"

Paulina **turned** to look. Sure enough, there was a shepherd leading his flock. Finally they'd found someone they could ask about **PROFESSOR SAGEFUR**!

The shepherd welcomed them with a friendly SMILE, which grew even **wider** when Paulina spoke to him in **Quechua***. He didn't have many opportunities to squeak with anyone, so he was happy to stop and chat.

"Yes, your friend the professor passed through here a few days ago. He was headed for the **tampu****, not too far away." He paused and looked up at the sky for a moment. "It would be wise for you to go there, too. A storm is headed this way!"

The shepherd raised his eyes to the sky again, to point out the dark rain clouds. Then he suddenly TURNED PALE and murmured: **"K-KUNTUR!"**

---

*Quechua was spoken by the Incas and is still spoken today by many people in South America. **A tampu is a roadside shelter.

Without squeaking good-bye, he herded his llamas together and led them away in a **HURRY**.

"What was that about?" asked Pamela, surprised. "What does *kuntur* mean?"

"In Quechua, it means '**condor**,'" explained Paulina.

She looked up at the sky, trying to figure out what had alarmed the shepherd. There was a condor circling above in between the **dark clouds**.

KUNTUR!

"I don't understand why he **SCURRIED** away like that. It's just a **condor**!"

"Well, we should **HURRY UP**, too, so we can reach that shelter. It's definitely going to start **raining** any minute," cried Violet.

Before she finished squeaking, it started to **pour**!

THE QUECHUA PEOPLE AND LANGUAGE

The Quechua people have lived in the Andes for centuries. Their language, also called Quechua, has survived both the Incan and Spanish conquerors. The language was in use long before the arrival of the Incas, who took advantage of its widespread use. They adopted Quechua and made it their own.

Today, Quechua is spoken by approximately six to eight million people in many areas of Peru, as well as parts of Colombia, Ecuador, Bolivia, and northeast Argentina.

PROFESSOR SAGEFUR

It took the Thea Sisters an hour to get to the tampu. The rain came down so hard, the mice couldn't see their paws when they held them up in front of their faces. Paulina drove at her SLOWEST pace, and she relied on the GPS to tell her which way to go. Twice their car got stuck in holes filled with WATER. Three times the mouselings had to get out and PUSH. Soon they were SOAKED to the fur!

"I'm not getting out anymore!" Colette decided. "Let's stop and wait for the rain to end!" Violet nodded in agreement. Her teeth were chattering from the COLD.

Suddenly, they saw a small light twinkling in front of them.

"The *tampu*!" exclaimed Pamela. EVERYONE BREATHED A SIGH OF RELIEF.

The mouselings climbed out of the car and raced toward the shelter. As soon as they entered, they saw an older mouse bending over the fireplace.

"PROFESSOR SAGEFUR!" called Paulina.

The professor was so **surprised**, he almost tripped over his tail. Seeing Paulina there was the last thing he expected!

"Well, tickle me with a cat-fur feather, it's Paulina! What are you doing here?!" he gasped.

"Professor, I'm here to help you look for **GONZALO**!" she responded.

She flung her paws around him, and the two of them hugged each other tight.

Paulina introduced the professor to all her friends, and they all settled down together.

Nicky lit the **FIRE** in the fireplace like a real camping expert. The mouselings took off their wet jackets and started drying off.

Paulina hurried back to the car to get a package from her luggage. It contained five hand-woven **ponchos*** and five brightly colored wool caps. She pawed them out to her friends.

"These are a present from Aunt Nidia. They are handmade from alpaca **WOOL**, and they're warmer than a tabby-trim coat!"

---

* A **poncho** is a large square of wool with a circular opening in the middle. It is worn over the head and around the shoulders.

HOT CHEESE SOUP

A nice warm meal put a little color back in **Violet's** PALE cheeks. Big bowls of soup with a lot of **hot** cheese were just what the five mouselings needed to warm up!

When they finished eating, they all gathered around the fireplace. It was time to **REVIEW** the situation.

"Tomorrow I want to hire someone from the area to be my guide. But it's **HARDER** than finding a cheese slice in a HAYSTACK," the professor said, sighing.

"Why?" asked Pamela.

"The local mice are all terrified of the **condor**!" he responded.

"The **KUNTUR** again!" murmured Colette.

"That happened to us, too, Professor!" explained Paulina. "We were asking a SHEPHERD for information, and he scurried away because he saw a condor!"

"That's exactly what I'm worried about," said PROFESSOR SAGEFUR. "Everyone in the countryside has been squeaking about a condor with a terrible CRY that has been chasing mice! Now FEAR has spread throughout these mountains faster than fleas on a feline, and no one wants to climb the peaks."

Paulina had a determined look on her snout. "We came all the way here to help you, Professor. Together we will find Gonzalo."

Professor Sagefur smiled. "Thank you, Paulina. I truly appreciate what you and your friends are trying to do for me."

"Do you have any idea where **GONZALO** was headed?" asked Violet.

The professor got a grave look on his snout. "Yes, I'm **AFRAID** so. He climbed Huayna Picchu! It is a very challenging summit. Gonzalo had trained well, but that **mountain** has gotten the best of better climbers."

Their heads filled with thoughts of Gonzalo and Huayna Picchu, the Thea Sisters went to get some rest.

HUAYNA PICCHU

Huayna Picchu, which means "young peak" in Quechua, is the mountain that towers over Machu Picchu. The path that leads to the peak is very rugged and hard to travel. The peak is about 8,900 feet above sea level.

A COURAGEOUS RODENT

The next morning, the sun was SHINING brightly. It looked as if all the MUD and PUDDLES would dry up quickly. But the road was a **mess**. Driving would be too DANGEROUS. Professor Sagefur and the Thea Sisters needed to proceed on paw. Professor Sagefur decided to find a few LLAMAS to carry the remaining food and equipment.

"Do we really need llamas?" asked Nicky. "We're as strong as pack rats! We can carry our own belongings."

The professor smiled. "I like your spirit, Nicky! But we're going to be climbing to a very high altitude, with a lot less oxygen than we're used to. It would be exhausting to scale those heights with even a VERY LIGHT backpack."

ANIMALS OF THE ANDES

CONDOR: The Andean condor is one of the biggest predatory birds in the world. It has a wingspan of almost ten feet and weighs between twenty and thirty pounds. It can reach an altitude of almost 15,000 feet.

CHINCHILLA: The chinchilla is a rodent with a pudgy body. Each one can grow to be up to fourteen inches long, not including the tail. Chinchillas use their back paws for hopping and their front paws for handling the roots and long grasses they eat. The chinchilla was hunted almost to extinction during the 1920s, but has since made a comeback thanks to protection laws.

PUMA: Pumas are also known as cougars or mountain lions. They are carnivores and belong to the feline family. They are very

good runners and jumpers — some have been known to jump eighteen feet from the ground into a tree! Pumas cannot roar, but they do make sounds that resemble whistles, squeaks, growls, and hisses.

ANDEAN (SPECTACLED) BEAR: This unusual-looking bear gets its name from the markings around its eyes, which resemble spectacles. These bears build platforms of leaves in trees, where they eat and sleep. They are very shy and tend to avoid humans, so there is still much we do not know about them.

CAMELS OF THE ANDES

Camelids are a family of mammals. In North Africa and Central Asia, camelids consist mostly of camels and dromedaries. In South America, however, they include the following:

LLAMA: The llama was domesticated by the Andean people thousands of years ago and prized for its milk, wool, meat, and even its waste, which was used to feed fires. The llama is a very strong animal — it can transport everything but humans.

ALPACA: Like the llama, the alpaca was domesticated thousands of years ago by people living in the Andes. Alpacas are smaller than llamas and are known for their soft, silky wool. Like llamas, they have very docile dispositions.

GUANACO: Guanacos are the ancestors of the llamas. They live in small groups in the wild. They are good runners and can reach speeds of forty miles an hour! Running in a pack is the guanaco's best defense against predators like pumas because the predators are unable to focus on any one animal.

VICUÑA: The vicuña is related to the llama, guanaco, and alpaca. It is the smallest of the family, and its dense, silky fur was once reserved for Incan nobility. Vicuñas travel in groups of females that are usually led by one male. When in danger, they emit a high-pitched whistle.

The vicuña and the guanaco are the only two camelids that cannot be domesticated.

While the professor was haggling over the price of the llamas, the mouselings made friends with two young shepherds. They were looking after what looked like baby llamas.

"These are alpacas," Paulina explained to her friends. "Try petting them. They're really soft!"

"They're adorable! And — ooh! — their fur is SOFTER than a calico cat's!" said Colette.

The shepherds laughed at Colette's amazement. Paulina decided to ask them

about GONZALO: Maybe one of them had seen him.

"Yes, I remember him," said the younger shepherd. "He is a cheerful and courageous rodent!"

"Courageous?" inquired Paulina. "What did he do to make you think he was courageous?"

The shepherd lowered his squeak and looked around **fearfully**. "**KUNTUR**! The condor zoomed down from the sky and headed straight for us! Its wings covered the **SUN**, and its cries made all my animals run away."

"What did Gonzalo do?" asked Paulina.

"He didn't **RUN**. He is a very **brave** rodent!"

"Then what?" asked Paulina. "What did he do next?"

The shepherd **shrugged**. "I don't know. I had to chase after my animals. But one thing is certain: If he escaped that condor, not only is he a courageous rodent, he's also **VERY LUCKY**!"

TOWARD HUAYNA PICCHU

The little group set out slowly, scampering in single file. Professor Sagefur was right: Even the slightest bit of effort was difficult for those who were not used to the **ALTiTUDE**. Without the llamas, they wouldn't have been able to bring all the equipment and **FOOD** they needed.

As the path climbed

higher, it became **NARROWER** and **ROCKIER**.

"This is an old Incan road," explained the professor. "Look at the **cobblestones**. Do you see the spot where they're not covered up by plants and shrubs? They are all placed together using the same technique. The Incas were a great people and wonderful builders."

"What do you think **GONZALO** is looking for up there on Huayna Picchu?" asked Paulina.

PROFESSOR SAGEFUR didn't answer right away. He stopped to check on the rest of the mouselings. Everyone was **TIRED**

except for Pamela and Paulina. "Some mice adapt more easily to the ALTITUDE than others," he told them.

Not far away was a clearing that was big enough to set up camp. "Let's stop here," the professor proposed. "We can rest and drink some hot tea, and I will tell you Gonzalo's story. Then we will set up the tents for NIGHTFALL."

When they had all settled in with their PIPING hot cups, the professor began to *tell the story*.

"Our tale begins a long time ago, in 1532, when the conquistadors arrived in PERU. They were under the command of Francisco Pizarro. The Spanish had never in their lives seen so many riches! They took Atahualpa, the emperor of the INCAS, as their PRISONER, and they forced the Incas

GOLD NECKLACE AND BUCKLE

to pay an enormouse ransom for him. So the Incas filled Atahualpa's entire cell with **GOLD**. Then they filled two more rooms with **SILVER**! All that was just a tiny portion of the immense **TREASURE** of the Incas. Most of it was hidden and never found again."

GOLD CHEST PLATE

TWO GOLD VASES

"And now **GONZALO** is **LOOKING** for the hidden treasure?" Paulina asked breathlessly.

GOLD MASK

The professor nodded. "The legend speaks of a SECRET CITY, **BUILT** in order to save the treasure from greedy invaders."

"A sort of **ENORMOUSE** safe!" interrupted Nicky.

Professor Sagefur smiled. "Exactly! Mice have searched for this safe for centuries. Hiram Bingham, the explorer, thought he had found it when he discovered Machu Picchu, but there was no trace of the treasure. After many DISAPPOINTMENTS, he ended up

believing that the Secret City was just a **LEGEND**."

"But your son doesn't believe that's true?" asked Colette.

The professor shook his snout. "Ever since he was little, **GONZALO** has dreamed of finding the Incas' treasure! He studied a lot and became an expert ARCHAEOLOGIST. His greatest fear is that the SECRET CITY will be found by UNSCRUPULOUS rodents. Some mice are capable of destroying important evidence of a great civilization if it means they can go home RICH. But GONZALO longs to discover the secret city not to become rich, but for the JOY of knowledge. Because, in the end, there is no wealth greater than knowledge! Remember this, mouselings: It is very important to discover the past if you want to understand the present."

The Thea Sisters nodded. They were impressed by the professor's devotion to knowledge.

Violet nudged Nicky. "Doesn't he remind you of Thea?" she whispered. "That sounds like something she would squeak."

SUSPENDED
IN THIN AIR!

Bright and early the next morning, the mouselings and Professor Sagefur set off together. Everyone had more **ENERGY** than a pack of rats at the World Cheese Convention. Even Colette, Nicky, and Violet were getting used to the altitude.

The path they were following **TWISTED** around the side of the **MOUNTAIN**. After many bends and turns, the explorers found themselves on the other side,

with a **vast** gorge in front of them.

There was no more **ROAD**. They'd reached the end of a high cliff! At the bottom of the gorge below was a **ROCKY** stream. There was only one way forward: on a NARROW bridge made of rope!

"Looks like we've reached the end of the line," declared Nicky.

"CHEWY CHEESE CURDS! I thought things like this only happened in the **movies**!" exclaimed Pamela.

"It's not as fragile as it looks," said Paulina. "I crossed one a few years ago, and it was much easier than I expected."

The suspended bridge was made of agave fiber threaded together into many cables. At its bottom, there was a NARROW platform of WOODEN planks designed to make crossing easier.

Paulina had already begun to step FORWARD, but PROFESSOR SAGEFUR stopped her. "Wait, Paulina! I'll go first! I want to see if it is as strong as it seems." The professor took a few QUICK steps. Soon he'd reached the center of the bridge. Suddenly, he began jumping up and down.

THUMP
THUMP
THUMP
THUMP
THUMP

SUSPENSION BRIDGES

The Inca were the only ancient American civilization to develop suspension bridges. At least 200 suspension bridges spanned river gorges when the conquistadors arrived in Peru. Some were 300 feet long! The bridges were made of cotton, grasses, saplings, and llama and alpaca wool. These fibers were braided and twisted together to make strong rope cables. The cables were replaced every other year to prevent sagging. Stringing the bridges across rivers and gorges was very dangerous, and many died in the process.

Colette, Nicky, Pamela, and Violet shot one another looks of bewilderment.

"What is he doing? Has he SHORTED A CIRCUIT in his brain?" Pamela exclaimed, PETRIFIED.

Nicky was stunned. "Does he think he's a kangaroo?"

"I think the cheese has slipped off his cracker," murmured Colette.

"STOP, PROFESSOR, STOP! IT'S DANGEROUS!" begged Violet. Her fur had turned as WHITE as mozzarella.

But the professor just laughed as he BOUNCED UP AND DOWN. "Don't worry, my little cheddar crisps!

THUMP THUMP THUMP

This bridge is solid. If a **stout** old mouse like me can use it as a **TRAMPOLINE**, it should be safe for us, the llamas, and all the equipment."

Suddenly, the professor noticed Violet's `pale` snout. "Are you all right, Violet? Are you afraid of heights?"

Violet was squeakless with **FRIGHT**. Her eyes were fixed on the bottom of the **ravine**. It was all she could do to nod.

PROFESSOR SAGEFUR scampered back to the mouselings and put a paw around Violet's shoulder. "Don't think about it! Help me make sure the packages on the llamas are balanced evenly. Meanwhile, your friends can go **AHEAD**!"

Paulina went first. She scampered forward **VERY SLOWLY** but without hesitation, keeping her steps even. When she'd reached the other side, she turned around and shouted encouragement to her friends. "You see? It hardly *rocks* at all!"

PROFESSOR SAGEFUR laughed. "Good job, Paulina! Now come on, mouselings, have courage! Let's hurry up. I'm as **hungry** as a mountain lion!"

Nicky and Colette were next. They looked a bit uncertain, but they went ahead.

Violet didn't feel ready yet. "Why don't you stay here with her?" the professor suggested to Pamela. "I'll take the llamas to the other side and then come back to get you."

The llamas seemed perfectly at ease on the **wobbly** bridge. One got a little **nervous** when the professor tried to put a rope around

its neck. Then it yanked itself free, spit in
PROFESSOR SAGEFUR'S snout, and crossed
the bridge in a hurry.

"Leaping llamas' legs!" sputtered the
professor, wiping his snout with one paw.
"That was truly AWFUL!"

Pamela burst out laughing, and even
Violet cracked a smile.

Slowly, Violet, Pam, and PROFESSOR
SAGEFUR stepped onto the bridge. From down

below, they could hear the **RUMBLE** of the angry river current.

"As you **walk**, try to think about something else," the professor advised Violet. "Concentrate on something NiCe!"

Violet nodded **NERVOUSLY**. She began humming a **SWEET** song that her grandmother **Lotus Flower** had always sung when she'd tucked Violet in for the night. **Despite herself, Violet smiled**.

Holding tight to that **HAPPY** memory, Violet took one **pawstep** at a time. Before long, she'd reached the other end of the bridge!

CA-CAAAAAAWWW!

The professor squeezed Violet's paw. "Great job, my dear! You did it! You were very *brave*!"

"Professor, come take a look!" Paulina called in a **LOUD SQUEAK**. She'd been looking for a good place to rest and she'd come across the remains of another campsite.

"Someone stopped here. Maybe it was **GONZALO**!" exclaimed Pamela.

"It could be . . . yes! These pawprints look fresh," confirmed the professor, examining the signs on the **GROUND**.

Just then, a deafening shriek came out of nowhere!

CA-CAAAAAAAAAAWWWWWWWWWWWWWWWW!

Professor Sagefur and the Thea Sisters pressed themselves up against the side of the cliff and covered their ears.

CA-CAAAAAAAAAAWWWWWWWWWWWWWWWW!

Terrified, the three llamas ran away.

CA-CAAAAAAAAAAWWWWWWWWWWWWWWWW!

What was making that terrible sound?

CA-CAAAAAAAAAAWWWWWWWWWWWWWWWW!

"It's the **KUNTUR**!" yelled Pamela, pointing toward the sky.

Behind the dark clouds that were covering the sun was the shadow of a bird. An ENORMOUSE bird!

"IT'S GOING TO ATTACK US!" cried Nicky.

"SEEK SHELTER, QUICKLY!" shouted the professor.

CA-CAAAAAAAAAAWWWWWWWWWWWWWWWW!

This time, the condor's cry was followed by a sinister *hiss*. But no one looked to see where it came from. They were running!

EVERYONE RACED FOR SHELTER AS FAST AS THEY COULD.

The mouselings and PROFESSOR SAGEFUR

were so busy scurrying away, they accidentally split up. Violet, Pam, and the professor turned right. After a few feet, they found shelter in a CAVE.

Nicky, Paulina, and Colette ran the other way, to the left. But they weren't as lucky as their friends. They couldn't find anywhere to hide! And the cries of the condor were getting closer and closer.

At last, Nicky, Paulina, and Colette saw some bushes and jumped into them. Before they realized what was happening, the ground CRUMBLED underneath their paws!

"HEEELLLLPPP!" yelled the mouselings.

HEEELLLPPPP!

All around them, it was D A R K E R than the inside of a cat's mouth.

The rock underneath their tails was moist from the **moss**. There was nothing to grab.

"I feel like I'm on a waterslide — without the water!" cried Nicky.

"How can you joke at a time like this?" cried Colette.

"Will . . . we . . . ever . . . hit . . . bottom?" Paulina wondered aloud as she bumped along.

Until suddenly . . . **THUMP!** Their long tumble was over at last.

For a few moments, there was only silence. Then, one at a time, the three mouselings began to squeak.

"**OOH, OOH, OOH!**" moaned Colette.

"Is everyone all right?" asked Paulina.

"**NO, OF COURSE NOT! NOTHING IS ALL RIGHT!!!!**" shouted Colette. "We've fallen into the middle of a **MUD PUDDLE**. My tail is all bruised. I think I tore a hole in my pants. And here's the straw that broke the llama's back — I broke a *pawnail*!"

A bright light shining at her snout silenced Colette. Nicky had pulled out her pocket FLASHLIGHT and was aiming it at her friend. "Oh, Colette, don't be such a **drama mouse**. Come on, get up!"

Paulina scrambled up and brushed herself off. "Let's see if we can figure out where we've ended up." She helped Colette up while Nicky led the **WAY**.

The light from the FLASHLIGHT was very dim, but, little by little, the mouselings' eyes got used to the D A R K. They advanced along a tunnel that was **narrow** but tall enough to stand up in. The walls were weirdly smooth. Even the ground seemed to be paved.

Despite the lack of light, Paulina, Nicky, and Colette scampered along quicker than gerbils on a treadmill.

"It almost seems as if someone dug this tunnel out of the **ROCK**," observed Paulina.

"You're right!" replied Nicky.

Just then, the flashlight's beam fell on a STATUE.

"**Holey cheese**, that's scary! What is it?" exclaimed Colette.

"It's an **INCAN** sculpture," said Paulina.

She stepped closer to get a better look.

"I wonder if it's some sort of guardian," mused Nicky.

"**A GUARDIAN** of *what*?" asked Paulina.

Nicky slowly aimed the FLASHLIGHT along the wall. At first, it appeared blank, but then she spotted an opening. "Of that **door**!" she gasped.

A STRANGE CONDOR

Meanwhile, the other group was huddled in the cave where they'd sought shelter from the condor.

CA-CAAAAAAWwwwwwwwwwww!

They could still hear its cries, but now they seemed to come from farther and farther away.

After a moment or two, Pamela cautiously approached the **CAVE** opening and peeked outside. "I think it's gone."

"Is it normal for a bird to make such **LOUD** sounds?" asked Violet. She was a little shaken.

Pam put her paw around her friend's shoulder. "I don't know, but it sure is **creepy**!"

Professor Sagefur frowned. "I hope Paulina and the other mouselings located another shelter. We must find them at once."

SCANNING the area around them, they crept out of the **CAVE**. There was no sign of the condor in the sky, but Violet noticed that the strange animal had left something near the cave's mouth. She bent down and picked up a black feather.

"A feather from the condor?" asked the professor.

"A feather, yes . . . but not from the condor!" said Violet. "This is a **RAVEN'S** feather!"

"Are you sure?" asked Professor Sagefur.

Pamela nodded. "Professor, when Violet says she knows something, you can bet your whiskers it's true! And hey, what's this?" She bent down and examined the **GROUND**.

She rested her paw on a dark splotch, then brought her fingers up to her snout. "But . . . this is motor oil!"

"**Motor oil?!**" Violet and the professor exclaimed.

"And it's still fresh!" said Pamela, nodding.

"But how could a car **CLIMB** all the way up here?"

"It couldn't," confirmed the professor.

"Are you thinking what I'm thinking?" asked Violet.

Pam nodded. "There's something not quite right about that **FLYING** condor," she concluded, scrutinizing the sky.

Professor Sagefur nodded in agreement. "*Someone* is trying to **SCARE US**!"

Violet **frowned**. "We've got to find Colette, Nicky, and Paulina right away!"

LET'S REVIEW!

How could a condor lose a raven's feather?!

Why is the condor making such loud, harsh cries? Condors are known to be silent birds.

Clue!

Where did the motor oil come from? Could it be from the condor?

AN UNEXPECTED ENCOUNTER

At the bottom of the dark hole, Paulina, Nicky, and Colette were getting ready to venture through the **door** they'd discovered.

In the **PITCH BLACK**, Nicky's small FLASHLIGHT was not very helpful. They caught a glimpse of a spacious room with walls covered with PICTURES.

Cheese niblets! Had the mouselings ended up in an Incan tomb?

Suddenly, a **SHADOWY FIGURE** flung itself at them!

"SQUEEEEEEEAK!" cried Colette.

Something struck Nicky's arm. The

flashlight fell from her paws and went out. They were in complete **DARKNESS**!

"No way!" cried Nicky. "It's like we're the three blind mice all over again!"

"Don't worry, I've got him!" **YELLED** Paulina.

Nicky and Colette tried to give her a paw, but they found themselves roughly shoved against the wall.

"**PAWS OFF THE FUR, YOU SLIMY SEWER RAT!**" yelled Colette, punching the air. She hit Paulina by accident. Caught off guard, Paulina let go of her captive.

The shadowy figure seized the opportunity to **RUN OFF**. But suddenly, the three mouselings heard a **THUD** and a cry of pain: "**OWWWW!!!**"

Then all was **quiet, quiet, quiet, quiet, quiet, quiet, quiet, quiet, quiet**.

At last, a thin sliver of light illuminated the scene. Nicky had found her FLASHLIGHT.

"Show me your snout, you cowardly tomcat!" she shouted, pointing it at him. Finally, Colette, Nicky, and Paulina had a good look at him.

"Why, it's GONZALO!!!" cried Paulina. Colette, Nicky, and PAULINA had found PROFESSOR SAGEFUR'S son!

DAD!

"P-Paulina?!" Gonzalo stuttered in surprise. For three seconds, the two of them stared at each other in silence, too **shocked** to squeak. Then they threw their paws around each other.

GONZALO was **HAPPY**. "Paulina, it's been so long since we last saw each other! I almost didn't recognize you!"

Colette was the first one to **BREAK UP** the happy reunion. "Sorry to interrupt, but I think it would be better to continue this conversation back outside, in daylight."

"**DITTO!**" exclaimed Nicky. "Let's get out of here!"

GONZALO gestured for the mouselings to follow him. Together, all four mice made their way down the **D A R K** tunnel.

"The **EXIT** is this way," explained Gonzalo. "You came in through the . . . er . . . **back door**."

Gonzalo, Colette, Nicky, and Paulina scampered along the long corridor, heading slightly uphill. After a few turns, they finally saw the light of day! They emerged right outside of the cave where Pamela, Violet, and the professor had found shelter.

"**Dad!**" cried Gonzalo.

"GONZALO!" exclaimed PROFESSOR SAGEFUR.

The professor and Gonzalo **hugged each other** tight. And so did Colette, Nicky, Pamela, Paulina, and Violet! They were RELIEVED to find one another safe and sound.

Paulina quickly introduced GONZALO to her four friends. There had been so much EXCITEMENT, PROFESSOR SAGEFUR suggested they make their campsite right where they were standing.

"It's time for some tea!" proposed Violet. She was eager to celebrate their reunion.

Unfortunately, the llamas had run away with all their food! And who could blame them? Everyone had been terrified by the condor's *MYSTERIOUS* attack.

"There's nothing to do but go on a **llama hunt**," Paulina said with a sigh.

Luckily, Nicky and Pamela found the llamas in a field nearby, grazing peacefully. Twenty minutes later, the group had all their equipment and **PROVISIONS**. They settled into their new campsite.

"You must forgive me for my behavior back there," said Gonzalo, sipping his tea. "In the **DARK**, I mistook you for my attackers."

"What attackers?" asked his father.

"Three nasty mice jumped me out of nowhere. I didn't realize it at the time, but

THEY STOLE EVERYTHING I HAD!

they'd been following me!" explained Gonzalo. "They stole everything I had, even my notebooks! And to think that I came so close to the SECRET CITY!"

"That's terrible!" cried Nicky.

"They were a real pack of cheeseheads," stated Gonzalo. "I fought with all my might, and eventually I was able to ESCAPE. I ran off and hid in a cave."

"That must be the same cave we hid in!" said Professor Sagefur.

"It certainly looks like it," said GONZALO. "That's where I discovered these OLD INCAN REMAINS. I found amazing

objects and **engravings**!"

"But why did you stay here?" asked his father. "You've been missing for two weeks! I didn't hear **A SQUEAK** out of you! I was so worried. Why didn't you turn around and ask for help?"

Gonzalo lowered his eyes. "I'm sorry, Dad! I didn't mean to worry you so much, but I really couldn't turn around! I needed to keep an **EYE** on those **RAT BURGLARS**. I wanted to find out who they were so I could report them. I was terrified they'd enter the **SECRET CITY**. And I wanted to be sure that they didn't ruin or rob the amazing **ANTIQUITIES** there!"

PROFESSOR SAGEFUR was silent. He had a stern look on his snout. "You are a *reckless* son, **GONZALO**, but you are a **GREAT** archaeologist!" he said at last, **SMILING**. "I'm proud of you."

THE SUSPICIOUS PLANS OF A SUSPICIOUS CHARACTER

"Were you able to find out who your attackers were?" asked Paulina.

GONZALO nodded. "They are Paco Manadunca's henchmice!"

"Paco Manadunca?! That sorry excuse for a rodent!" exclaimed PROFESSOR SAGEFUR. He had turned bright red with indignation. "He's an archaeologist, too," he explained to the Thea Sisters.

Gonzalo nodded. "Professor Manadunca is an ARCHAEOLOGIST who is very highly regarded by many. But my father and I have long suspected that he's sneaky and DISHONEST."

"Still, I never would have thought that he would be capable of something like **this**," Professor Sagefur said, shaking his snout.

"You wouldn't have been able to do anything, Dad," said Gonzalo. "Manadunca is greedy, disloyal, and dangerous. He's been **spying** on me ever since I found the *quipu*. He pretended to be excited about my research!"

He pretended to be excited about my research!

"Oh, yes, excited enough to steal it!" Professor Sagefur's whiskers were SHAKING with rage.

"Excuse me . . . but what is the KiP . . . the CHiP . . . you know, what you said?"

QUIPU

The Incas had a very unusual way of keeping records. Instead of writing numbers on paper, on papyrus, or on tablets, the Incas made knots with multicolored ropes. If the *quipu* were a calculator, the knots would correspond to numbers. In fact, the word *quipu* means "knots." Using their *quipu*, the Incas were able to perform very quick and precise calculations.

Thanks to the *quipu*, every Incan governor was able to register the number of people who lived in his territory and how much tax money was owed to the state.

THE INCAS DID NOT HAVE anything that the people of today RECOGNIZE AS WRITING.

THE *quipu* were made from a series of multicolored ropes with knots on them. They were used to count, but some historians believe they were also used to compose and preserve epic poems and legends.

The number and position of the knots as well as the color of each cord indicated different things.

It is very hard to interpret the quipu. The meaning of the knots and colors remains a mystery. Perhaps a gold string was used to mean the sun or the Incan king.

CLUES

1

THE CONDOR

2

OIL

MOTOR OIL

3

THE FEATHER

interjected Pamela.

"*Quipu* is the **INCAN** form of record keeping," explained **GONZALO**.

"You found a *quipu*?" asked Paulina.

"Yes, I was **LUCKY** enough to find a *quipu* that **reveals** the location of the **SECRET CITY**. But somehow **Manadunca** got his **greedy paws** on my notes. He followed me up here to **STEAL** my discovery!"

Pamela took out the raven's **feather**, which she'd been keeping in her **pocket**. "Gonzalo, is there a condor in your story? One that squawks like a loudsqueaker, spits out **motor oil**, and is covered in raven's feathers?"

"AREN'T YOU A SMARTYPAWS, PAMELA!" said Gonzalo, beaming at her.

"That's great, but, um, would you be so kind as to explain it to us, too?" asked Colette, who was having trouble keeping up with all the **NEWS**.

"Yes, please do!" said PROFESSOR SAGEFUR. "What does **Manadunca** have to do with the condor?"

"It's not a real condor! It's a **MOTORIZED** hang glider disguised as a condor," explained Gonzalo. "**Manadunca** and his henchmice have covered it in **feathers**.

4

CONDOR-SHAPED GLIDER

They're using it to SCARE the local mice!"

"But why?" asked Colette.

"Once Manadunca discovered the location of the SECRET CITY, he wanted to keep CURIOUS mice away!" said Gonzalo. "He was sure he'd be able to get in easily."

"But if they are still using the fake condor to scare rodents away, that must mean that Manadunca hasn't found what he was looking for!" Violet squeaked slowly.

"Your friends are really brainy, Paulina!" exclaimed GONZALO. "That's right: He wasn't able to find the city on his own! That's why Manadunca had his henchmice ATTACK me and steal my notebooks. But my notes don't explain how to open the DOOR OF THE SUN, which is the only way to get into the SECRET CITY."

"It would probably be easier for him to

Professor Paco Manadunca

Professor Manadunca is an unscrupulous archaeologist. His full name is Paco Felipe Manadunca. One of his ancestors arrived in Peru with the Spanish conquistadors.

destroy the door than to open it!" blurted **PROFESSOR SAGEFUR**.

At his words, everyone fell silent. It was as if the **SHADOW** of an **ENORMOUSE** cat had fallen over them.

"Yes, a slimy sewer rat like Manadunca would stop at nothing if it meant he could get his hands on the hidden **INCAN** treasure," said Gonzalo.

"It sounds like you think he would even destroy the **SECRET CITY**!" cried Paulina.

"I still don't quite understand," said Colette. "Where exactly *is* the Secret City?"

Gonzalo pointed up. "It's right there!"

Nicky **leaped** to her paws. "Well, what are we waiting for? Let's go stop him!"

THE DOOR
OF THE SUN

Inspired by Nicky's words, the Thea Sisters, Gonzalo, and the professor left the cave and scurried back along the **PATH**. Soon they'd arrived at the foot of a **stairway**. Above them stood the walls of the Secret City! What an extraordinary sight!

"No one but us has seen this in almost five hundred years," breathed Paulina.

At the center of the walls, the Door of the Sun **GLEAMED** like a beacon. It had been closed for centuries, protecting the Incan **TREASURES** that lay within.

Manadunca's shrill **squeak** echoed down from above. The Sagefurs and the mouselings exchanged looks of **dismay**. They could just make out what he was saying, and it confirmed their **WORST FEARS**.

Paco Manadunca had decided to knock down the **DOOR OF THE SUN**!

Manadunca had tried every which way to open it. He'd even tried waiting for Gonzalo to get there, in hopes that his notes would contain the solution to the **ENIGMA**. But no! The door refused to open.

"Enough! I'm sick of this rat race!" he shouted. "What do I care if I break a door down? There are treasures much more precious than this strip of **GOLD** in there!"

Manadunca and his three henchmice decided to set up three small piles of **EXPLOSIVES** at the bottom of the door.

THERE WAS NO TIME TO LOSE!

"We must **stop** them!" cried the Professor.

"I think I have an idea," said Paulina.

The little group huddled together for some

frantic squeaking. Soon, a plan emerged: Gonzalo would get Manadunca's attention while the Thea Sisters and the professor, who would be HIDING close by, would prepare a big surprise for them!

PROFESSOR SAGEFUR clasped GONZALO'S paw. "Are you ready, son?"

"I'm ready. I won't let you down, Dad!" With that, Gonzalo scampered up the stairs.

"Wait, Paco!" he shouted, running up the last steps. "I won't let you destroy that door!"

Manadunca and his henchmice were so startled, they practically jumped out of their fur. But when they saw that GONZALO was alone, they smirked at one another.

"And who's going to stop me?" **sneered** Manadunca. "You?!"

"I'll **REPORT** you!" replied GONZALO. "All of PERU will find out that you're nothing more than a **LOUSY** rat burglar!"

"**Get him!**" ordered Manadunca, and his henchmice **sprang** at Gonzalo.

But **GONZALO** was one pawstep ahead of them. He raced to one side, toward the **ROCKS**, and made a flying leap into some bushes. Then he **scurried** away, crashing through the tangled **vines** and **BRANCHES**.

Unfortunately, the henchmice were gaining on him. They were about to **nab** him when they stumbled over a **TRIP ROPE**! The three thugs **collapsed** in a heap.

Before they had a moment to realize what was going on, the Thea Sisters jumped on them, and the henchmice were tied up like **flies** in a SpiderWeb!

As for Paco Manadunca, Professor Sagefur saw to him: He roped him with a **lasso**. Manadunca was angrier than a LION ON A LEASH!

A DOOR . . . WITHOUT A LOCK?

Now that Manadunca and his henchmice were out of commission, it was up to Gonzalo and his father to open the Door of the Sun!

The Thea Sisters stared at the door in awe. "I don't think I've ever seen anything so fabumouse," breathed Colette.

Along the sides were two **IDENTICAL** handles. Pamela reached toward one, but **PROFESSOR SAGEFUR** quickly stopped her. "Nobody touch them! They could spring a **BOOBY TRAP**."

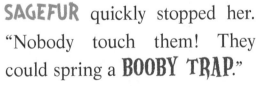

"This is quite a **DILEMMA!**" said Violet. "If we make the wrong choice, we could end up in real trouble!"

Paulina smiled thoughtfully. "The solution could be much simpler than we think. This situation reminds me of the fable of the evil king and the clever prisoner that my mother used to tell me when I was little! I loved that

Once upon a time, there was an evil king who took many prisoners. In his kingdom, it was tradition that one prisoner would be freed every year, during the Festival of the Sun. But the king had no use for that tradition, so he thought up a way to trick his subjects.

The king said to one prisoner, " will put a ball of gold under on vase and a ball of silver unde another. If you can guess wher the piece of gold is, I will free yo Otherwise you will stay in jail!"

STORY. I never got tired of listening to it."

The other mouselings and the two ARCHAEOLOGISTS gathered around to listen to PAULINA tell the **tale**.

The king was very tricky. He put a piece of silver under both of the vases. There was no gold piece at all!

The prisoner realized he was being tricked, but he couldn't accuse the king of cheating! He had to choose one of the vases.

RIDDLE:
How did the prisoner save himself?
Turn the page to find the answer.

"So?" said Nicky eagerly. "How was the 𝙿𝚁𝙸𝚂𝙾𝙽𝙴𝚁 able to save himself?"

"Chewy **cheese dumplings**, I think I've got it!" cried Violet. "He just chose one of the vases and said there was **SILVER** under it."

"VIOLET'S RIGHT!" said Paulina. "The prisoner pointed to one of the two vases and said, 'There is a ball of **SILVER** under this one! So the piece of **GOLD** must be under the other one.' He lifted the vase and showed everyone the ball of silver. Then the king was

"This is the vase with the ball of silver!"

The prisoner outsmarted the king!

forced to free him, because if he'd revealed that there was no ball of **GOLD** under the other vase, he would have exposed his **trick**!"

The professor laughed. "Very clever! The only way not to call the king a **LIAR** would be to choose one of the vases. Either of them! And we will do the same thing with these handles that are here to **trick** us: It doesn't matter which handle we pick. We can choose **either**!"

PROFESSOR SAGEFUR placed his right paw on one of the handles and turned it slowly. He heard something release: CLACK!

At first, nothing happened. Then the **GROUND** started to tremble and ancient gears began to turn.

CREAK . . . CREAK . . . CREEAAAAK!!!

Very, very slowly, the door creaked open!

"This is so exciting," whispered Pamela.

GONZALO turned to Manadunca. "You are a **LIAR** and a **THIEF**, but you are still an archaeologist, and this is an extremely important moment for ARCHAEOLOGY. It is only right that you come with us."

GONZALO and Pamela made sure that Manadunca's henchmice were safely **tied up**. Then the little group crossed the threshold of the **DOOR OF THE SUN**!

iNSiDE THE
SECRET CiTY

The door opened into a semicircular room. From there, three corridors extended in different directions. A faint **LIGHT** shone down from small windows near the roof.

"*But where is the real city?*" asked Colette. "*Where are all the streets and buildings?*"

"It isn't a real city," explained **GONZALO**. "No one has ever lived here. This place was used only to protect the treasure."

"So I'm guessing the **TREASURE** won't be right at our pawtips, will it?" said Nicky.

"You know how to find it, don't you, son?" the professor asked Gonzalo.

But the answer wasn't what his father was expecting: "No, Dad. I don't have a **CLUE**!"

"How could that be, Gonzalo?!" **PROFESSOR**

SAGEFUR cried in surprise. "You brought us all the way here for NOTHING?"

GONZALO shrugged. "We'll have to put our best paw forward. The treasure is most likely hidden within the LABYRINTH. Back in ancient times, the Incas built elaborate mazes to hide their TREASURES. We'll have to try not to get LOST, and I have an idea how to prevent that from happening!"

Gonzalo took a long rope from Manadunca's EQUIPMENT. They would use it to mark the path they had already taken so they could find their way back.

Gonzalo turned to face his friends. "Keep your eyes open! There could be TRAPS!"

They set out through the door in the middle. Gonzalo quickly untied Manadunca. "Now that we're so close to the treasure, I know you won't try to RUN AWAY."

Labyrinth is another word for *maze* — a network of passages that is so complicated, it's almost impossible to find the way out. Legend has it that King Minos of Crete ordered the inventor Daedalus to build the first labyrinth. The king intended to keep the Minotaur, a monster with a human body and bull's head, hidden away in the labyrinth.

According to Greek myth, Minos demanded that the city of Athens give him seven maidens and seven young men to sacrifice to the Minotaur. The son of the Athenian king, Theseus, joined forces with the city's young people to destroy the monster. Minos's daughter, Ariadne, fell in love with Theseus and told him the secret of the labyrinth. She gave Theseus a ball of thread that was long enough to last through the whole length of the labyrinth. After he defeated the Minotaur, Theseus used this gift to escape along with the other Athenians.

The little group soon found themselves at their first CROSSROADS, and GONZALO decided which path to take. As they made their way through the maze, he unraveled the rope to mark the ROAD they'd taken.

Professor Sagefur and Manadunca followed close behind him. Next came the five Thea Sisters. When a wall BLOCKED their path, they were able to change direction without getting confused, thanks to the rope.

The labyrinth's corridors

Help!!!

were tall and narrow, with small windows near the roof. The group stayed in the shadows.

They could just barely make out the pictures that decorated the walls. The ground was covered with **COLORED** stones.

Thus far, they hadn't encountered any **BOOBY TRAPS**. It seemed like they weren't in any danger, until ... **THUMP**!

Manadunca tripped on a stone that was slightly higher than the others. With a mighty **RUMBLE**, the ground began to open up.

The stones at his paws crumbled, revealing an ENORMOUSE abyss. Where there had been ground before, now there was an endless PIT.

"Watch the gap!" cried Nicky. She spotted a LEDGE inside the wall and THREW herself at it. All the mouselings leaped after her. They were safe!

But Manadunca was not. "HELP!!!" he shouted. He was hanging on to the edge of the abyss with one paw.

GONZALO reached for him. "Grab my paw!"

With the professor's help, GONZALO was able to pull him to safety. Now, however, there was another problem: The mouselings were on the other side.

THEY WERE SEPARATED!

THE SIMPLEST IDEAS . . .

"Wait here!" Gonzalo shouted to the Thea Sisters. "We will continue with the help of the rope. We'll come back and get you as soon as we can!"

With that, the three ARCHAEOLOGISTS disappeared into the intricate LABYRINTH once more.

But the mouselings soon spotted the flaw in Gonzalo's plan.

"Maybe the right DIRECTION is the one on our side!" said Pamela.

"If we keep going, we might even find another exit," added Nicky.

"I say, let's **keep going**!" said Violet. "But how will we make sure we don't get lost?"

"Good point, Vi. We don't have a rope," Colette observed **sadly**.

Paulina thought it over. Then she took out a small notebook and a pen from her pack. "We'll use this!" she said. "At every **CROSSROADS**, I'll write down whether we turned *left* or **right**. That way, if we need to turn back, we can **AVOID** the **ROADS** that we were already on!"

As soon as they reached the first fork, Paulina wrote down a number and a letter: **1R**. "What does that mean?" asked Violet.

"First fork, right," responded Paulina. "**1L** would mean first fork, left. **2R** for the second fork, right, and so on . . ."

"**FABUMOUSE!**" Pamela exclaimed, squeezing Paulina's paw. "The simplest ideas are the ones that work best. You're a **genius**!"

YOU'RE A GENIUS!

THEY WERE READY TO KEEP GOING.

THE SIGN OF THE JAGUAR

Meanwhile, **GONZALO**, **PROFESSOR SAGEFUR**, and **Manadunca** were scurrying down the intricate hallways in the opposite direction from the five mouselings. Their path was becoming even more twisty and winding, with STAIRS that went UP and DOWN.

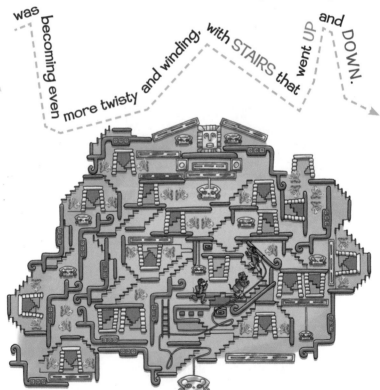

To: Gabby

From: Dad

...ewil Perfect

After a little while, they ran out of *rope*!

"What now?" asked **Manadunca**. "How can we continue without getting lost in the **LABYRINTH**?"

"Let's try following these **PICTURES**," suggested Gonzalo. "Near every fork, there is a picture of a **JAGUAR'S** head. All the heads seem to be facing the same direction. We can follow them like arrows."

"What if we end up at a **DEAD END**?" asked **Manadunca**.

GONZALO shrugged. "Then we'll turn back and head in the **OPPOSITE DIRECTION**."

They continued along the path. **GONZALO** and the professor were confident

We'll follow these!

they'd figured out the best way to proceed. At every **CROSSROADS**, there was a picture of a **JAGUAR**.

After a little while, they noticed that the **JAGUAR'S** heads were always looking left. And, in fact . . . they ended up right where they had **STARTED**! The end of the *rope* was there on the ground waiting for them.

AROUND LIKE RATS IN A MAZE! THEY HAD SPUN

TRAPPED!

Colette, **Nicky**, Pamela, PAULINA, and **Violet** were having problems, too. Going forward was very difficult! The **LABYRINTH** was really complicated. Plus, they were afraid another **TRAP** would open under their paws, as had happened to **Manadunca**.

The Thea Sisters proceeded in single file, stepping only on the **ROCKS** that Paulina, who was leading them, had stepped on.

"We're moving slower than a **fat** cat after a lunchtime feast!" complained Colette.

The **LABYRINTH** was testing their NERVES and their patience, but the worst was still to come. Suddenly, they heard a **STRANGE** sound.

HISSSSSSSSSSSSSSSSSSSSSSSSSSSSSSSS!

"**Uh-oh**, what was that?" asked Violet, alarmed. The five mouselings looked around, but they didn't see anything **unusual**.

Then something **HIT** them. And then **SOMETHING** else. And **ANOTHER**. And still **ANOTHER**!

An avalanche of **CLAY BALLS** was raining down on the mouselings! They were coming from every direction.

PLUNK PLUNK PLUNK PLUNK PLUNK PLUNK

The five Thea Sisters dashed out of the room as **BALLS** poured down on them.

They scurried out the only exit they spotted. Immediately, a DOOR SLID DOWN FROM THE CEILING, closing them in!

They found themselves locked in a tiny, DARK room without doors or windows. "WE'RE TRAPPED!" cried Paulina.

DOWN THE CHUTE

On the other side of the abyss, frustration was mounting. "WE'RE RIGHT BACK WHERE WE STARTED FROM," blurted PROFESSOR SAGEFUR.

"Hmm, following the jaguar's faces didn't lead us anywhere. Maybe we should try the OPPOSITE direction," GONZALO said thoughtfully.

Manadunca nodded impatiently. "The important thing is that we get to the TREASURE!"

They scampered forward AS QUICKLY AS POSSIBLE. The professor was worried it would be DARK soon. Without light coming from the windows, they wouldn't be able to SEE and would have to STOP. Fortunately, the path was getting easier to follow, and the hallways were getting wider and **brighter**. There weren't any more **STAIRS**, just a slight upward slope.

"Maybe this is the right way!" **GONZALO** said hopefully.

"The **TREASURE** can't be far!" declared Manadunca.

"**THERE!**" shouted **PROFESSOR SAGEFUR**. In front of them was a beautifully decorated door that was identical to the **DOOR OF THE SUN**.

"I'll bet it opens the same way as the other one!" said GONZALO.

He put his paw on one of the handles. Suddenly, the door BURST OPEN! Manadunca, who was behind the other two, PUSHED through them. He wanted to be first to the TREASURE.

No such luck. ALL THREE OF THEM ENDED UP ON AN ENORMOUSE SLIDE.

Down, down, down, down, down, down, down they slid. . . .

THE SECRET DOOR

"I can't believe we're **TRAPPED**!" sputtered Violet.

"There must be a way out of here! There's got to be!" cried Colette.

Pamela was despairing. "This is worse than the time I got my paw stuck in a glue trap," she said, sighing.

"How are we going to get out of here?" asked Paulina. For the first time, she looked **glum**.

Nicky was so **WORRIED**, she didn't squeak a word. She just leaned her shoulders against the wall, trying to figure out what to do next.

As she did, she thought she felt the

WALL behind her *MOVE*. Was it possible?

Nicky touched the wall again. It seemed just like the others, but when she touched it she realized it was different from the other walls in the **LABYRINTH**. It wasn't made of STONE.

"Moldy Brie, it's **WOOD**!" exclaimed Nicky. "I mean, it's a **FAKE WALL**!"

The mouselings all gathered around to touch the wall.

"It's really made of wood!" said Pamela, tapping it with one paw. It sounded HOLLOW.

"This must be a **SECRET DOOR**. See how it's **PAINTED** to look like the others? I'll bet it hides a **SECRET** passageway!" declared Paulina.

Colette pushed on the wall with all her might. It **shook**, but it didn't move. "But how do we get it open?"

"I have an **idea**!" said Violet. She tried something a little different: using her **PAWS** to move the wall to one side. "Maybe it's a sliding door," she explained.

Violet's intuition was right: The door slid sideways. In front of them was the most important hallway of all.

"This way to the **TREASURE**!" shouted Paulina. All five mouselings jumped up and down and hugged one another in **JUBILATION**.

OUCHIE! OUCH! TRIPLE OUCH!

Meanwhile, the professor, Gonzalo, and Manadunca were sliding at full speed down the labyrinth's latest booby trap.

"**HEELLLLP!**" they shouted.

The slide was becoming steeper and steeper. At last, it ended, and they tumbled out into the open. They found themselves in broad daylight again, outside the Secret City.

"So much for the treasure," **groaned** Gonzalo. "I can't believe three experienced archaeologists like us fell for that trap!"

"Ouchie! Ouch! Triple ouch with cheese on top!" complained PROFESSOR SAGEFUR.

They'd landed in the middle of some prickly shrubs, and he was having trouble getting out of them.

Gonzalo scrambled up and gave his father a paw. "Are you okay, Dad?"

"Oh, don't worry. Nothing's **BROKEN**, son!" his father assured him. "When I was a little mouse, the slide was my **FAVORITE** thing at the playground, but I am definitely too old for it now!" He laughed.

Meanwhile, **Manadunca** had *rolled* much farther down than the other two. He realized that Gonzalo and the professor weren't paying him any attention.

So he took the opportunity to slip away. What a sneaky **RAT!**

IN THE
TREASURE ROOM

Back inside the SECRET CITY, Colette, Nicky, Pamela, PAULINA, and **Violet** were scampering toward the treasure room. They could just make it out at the end of a short corridor.

Paulina was in the lead, with her four friends right behind her. As the Thea Sisters peeked into the treasure room, their EYES grew as round as wheels of Swiss cheese. It was an **enormouse** room, held up by tall pillars. The walls were covered with colorful pictures. The ceiling was midnight blue, and it looked like an enchanting STARRY SKY.

OOOH!

The room was filled with gorgeous objects, all placed there with great care. The mouselings didn't know where to LOOK first. In one corner, there were BEAUTIFUL vases. In another, there was some strange EQUIPMENT; in another, there were fabrics and looms. And everywhere, there were closed jars.

There was a lot of DUST and spiderwebs, of course, but most of the objects had resisted the damage of time. They seemed almost perfectly preserved. The room felt more like the centerpiece of an incredible MUSEUM than an enormouse safe that was more than five hundred years old. It was like peering

through a window from the present into the **PAST**.

Colette, Nicky, Pam, Paulina, and Violet scattered about the great room. They were fascinated by all the marvels it contained.

"Crusty kitty litter, **what strange treasure**!" exclaimed Paulina.

"It's true!" admitted Pamela, looking around. "There are no treasure chests filled with gold and precious gems."

"Only vases, statues, and fabumouse fabrics," said Colette, turning slowly around to get a better **LOOK** at everything.

Paulina, meanwhile, was gazing at the pictures on the walls. The colors were still

BRIGHT and the **images** were clear, as if they'd been painted yesterday instead of centuries ago. The paintings depicted scenes from Incan daily life.

doing housework . . .

"Look at all the *quipu*!" exclaimed Violet, who had found a chest filled to the brim with **knotted** ropes, placed there with great care.

Violet and Paulina only needed to glance at it to know: "*This* is the REAL TREASURE!" declared Violet.

and laboring in craftsmice's workshops.

"A **priceless** treasure!" agreed Paulina.

The other mouselings

stared at them, not comprehending.

"The INCAS preserved the **HISTORY** of their entire civilization," explained Paulina. "All their knowledge is here!"

"They saved the expertise of their builders, who were able to **LIFT** stone walls to the top of the Andes!" said Violet, pointing to a picture of workers building a temple.

"They saved the knowledge of their **ASTRONOMERS**, who studied the stars without telescopes!" continued Paulina, gazing at the ceiling.

THEY SAVED THE EXPERTISE OF THEIR BUILDERS.

THEY SAVED THE KNOWLEDGE OF THEIR ASTRONOMERS.

"They even saved their beauty secrets!" interjected Colette. "There are wonderful perfumes in these bottles! Even more fragrant than Mousey Sighs!"

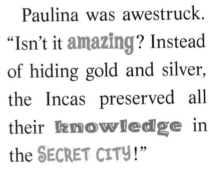

THEY EVEN SAVED THEIR BEAUTY SECRETS!

Paulina was awestruck. "Isn't it amazing? Instead of hiding gold and silver, the Incas preserved all their knowledge in the SECRET CITY!"

"PROFESSOR SAGEFUR was right! Knowledge is truly the GREATEST TREASURE!" said Pamela.

Nicky nodded.

"THE INCAS REALLY WERE EXTRAORDINARY!"

A LITTLE SPIN . . .

Getting out of the **LABYRINTH** was much easier and *QUICKER* than getting in. The rainstorm of **clay balls** had ended. And as it turned out, the gate that had closed behind them was made of rotting **WOOD**.

When the Thea Sisters scampered through the **DOOR OF THE SUN**, they found PROFESSOR SAGEFUR and GONZALO waiting for them. The two archaeologists could hardly contain their *excitement* when they heard about the room the mouselings had discovered.

The great news of the found treasure was only slightly marred by Manadunca's escape.

"I was so **angry** when I realized he was gone! I never should have let him come with us," **GONZALO** admitted regretfully. "We'll never be able to find him again."

"I think I know a way we could catch him!" said Pamela, tossing her tail over her shoulder. She'd noticed a strange pile of branches near the **DOOR OF THE SUN**. She moved them out of the way and . . .

"Putrid cheese puffs, it's the **giant condor**!" exclaimed Violet.

Hidden in the bushes was the fake condor that had caused such **FEAR** among the local

THE FAKE CONDOR!

mice. Once they saw it up close, it didn't look scary at all. It was just a simple **MOTORIZED** glider, covered in raven's feathers and with a fake condor's head.

Pamela didn't hesitate for a moment. She climbed into the pilot's seat.

Violet was alarmed. "What are you doing, Pam?" she **SCREAMED**.

"Just taking her out for a little **spin**!" Pamela answered **cheerfully**. Then she turned on the motor. A moment later, she was **SOARING** through the air!

Meanwhile, that **scoundrel** Paco Manadunca was crossing the rope bridge. He thought he'd escaped free and clear. "Those **cheddarheads** will never find me out here!" He still had a lot of walking to do, but the most important thing was that he wouldn't end up in **JAIL**!

Suddenly, a terrible SHRIEK made his fur stand on end.

CA-CAAAAAAAAAWWWWWWWWWWWWWWWW!

Manadunca couldn't believe it. It sounded just like the shriek from his condor-glider!

But if his henchmice were still tied up outside the SECRET CITY, **WHO WAS FLYING IT**?

Manadunca turned on one paw and looked up at the sky. But he lost his balance and found himself hanging in midair, with his snout down and his paws tangled in the *ropes*!

"*HEEEEEELLLPPPPP!*" he shrieked.

Slowly but surely, the ropes were fraying. Manadunca was thrashing about, which didn't help.

"*HEEEEEELLLPPPPP!*" he shouted. "I'M GOING TO FAAAAAALLLLLLL!!!"

Pamela steered the glider into a nosedive under the bridge just as Manadunca started to **FALL**.

THUMP!

Manadunca landed right on top of the glider.

A NEW THEA SISTER!

The mouselings and the two Sagefurs turned **Paco Manadunca** and his three henchmice over to the Cuzco **POLICE**. Professor Sagefur and his son, Gonzalo, told the world the extraordinary news:

INCREDIBLE!

FOUND: The Secret City of the Incas!

The news made the **FRONT PAGE** on newspapers and **websites** around the world.

When the **mouselings**, **PROFESSOR SAGEFUR**, and **GONZALO** returned to **MACHU PICCHU**, they found **Maria** waiting for them. Maria and Paulina threw their paws around each other.

MARIA WAS BESIDE HERSELF WITH HAPPINESS.

"I've been tracking you the whole time!" she cried. "And you never made a false move. Paulina, you're sharper than a block of NEW YORK CHEDDAR!"

Paulina laughed and HUGGED her sister.

After she'd greeted Paulina, Maria wanted to kiss everyone. When she got to Violet, she took a small pumpkin from her bag and said, "Frilly is doing well, but I think he misses you."

Violet took the pumpkin gratefully. "Thank you, Maria. I knew I could count on you!" Then she turned to her friends.

"I think Maria deserves to be a Thea Sister, don't you?"

"Yes!" "All right!" "Of course!" "Hooray!" the mouselings cheered.

Maria was so happy! "Thank you! Thank you so much! I promise I won't let you down."

PAULINA put a paw around her little sister. "We know you won't, sis. You've **earned** this."

When they reached CUZCO, the Thea Sisters were received like heroes. A huge **celebration** was thrown in their honor. The **GREEN MICE** came, and so did half of Cuzco. In fact, **Maria** was the one to send out the **cheeseVite**!!!

A GIFT FOR MARIA

I had read the entire fabumouse story of my friends' ADVENTURE in one sitting. It was already deep into the night. That meant because of the time difference, it was the perfect time to call Peru! I was tired, but I just couldn't miss this opportunity to squeak with the Thea Sisters.

After I'd chatted with the mouselings and told them how proud I was of them, I asked to speak to **Maria**.

"I'm going to write a book about the adventure of the SECRET CITY," I told her. "As soon as it's published, I'll send you a copy. That way, when you read the story, you can relive it along with your big sister!"

Maria was touched. "Thanks, Thea! I

can't wait to come to Mouseford
Academy and be a Thea Sister, too!"

I just knew that little mouseling would
grow up to be just as SMART, **brave**,
and LOYAL as her sister! I couldn't wait
to become her teacher, too.

They were more than friends. They were sisters!

THEA SISTERS

Want to read the next adventure
of the Thea Sisters?
I can't wait to tell you all about it!

THEA STILTON AND THE
MYSTERY IN PARIS

When Colette invites her friends to come
home with her to Paris for spring break,
the five mice are delighted. While they're in
France, they'll even get to attend Colette's
fashion-designer friend Julie's runway show
at the Eiffel Tower! But soon after the Thea
Sisters arrive, Julie's designs are stolen. Will
the five mice be able to catch the thief in time
to save the fashion show?

And don't miss any of my other fabumouse adventures!

THEA STILTON AND THE DRAGON'S CODE

THEA STILTON AND THE MOUNTAIN OF FIRE

THEA STILTON AND THE GHOST OF THE SHIPWRECK

THEA STILTON AND THE SECRET CITY

Want to read my next adventure?
I can't wait to tell you all about it!

THE PECULIAR
PUMPKIN THIEF

Halloween is a few days away when
all of the pumpkins in New Mouse
City disappear! There's a thief on
the loose, and the thief wants to stop
Halloween. Can my detective friend
Hercule Poirat and I solve the mystery
in time to save Halloween?

And don't miss any of my other fabumouse adventures!

#1 LOST TREASURE OF THE EMERALD EYE

#2 THE CURSE OF THE CHEESE PYRAMID

CAT AND MOUSE IN A HAUNTED HOUSE

#4 I'M TOO FOND OF MY FUR!

#5 FOUR MICE DEEP IN THE JUNGLE

#6 PAWS OFF, CHEDDARFACE!

RED PIZZAS FOR A BLUE COUNT

#8 ATTACK OF THE BANDIT CATS

#9 A FABUMOUSE VACATION FOR GERONIMO

#10 ALL BECAUSE OF A CUP OF COFFEE

IT'S HALLOWEEN, YOU 'FRAIDY MOUSE!

#12 MERRY CHRISTMAS, GERONIMO!

#13 THE PHANTOM OF THE SUBWAY

#14 THE TEMPLE OF THE RUBY OF FIRE

#15 THE MONA MOUSA CODE

#16 A CHEESE-COLORED CAMPER

#17 WATCH YOUR WHISKERS, STILTON!

#18 SHIPWRECK O THE PIRATE ISLAN

#19 MY NAME IS STILTON, GERONIMO STILTON

#20 SURF'S UP, GERONIMO!

#21 THE WILD, WILD WEST

#22 THE SECRET OF CACKLEFUR CASTLE

A CHRISTMAS TALE

#23 VALENTINE'S DAY DISASTER

#24 FIELD TRIP TO NIAGARA FALLS

#25 THE SEARCH FOR SUNKEN TREASURE

#26 THE MUMMY WITH NO NAME

#27 THE CHRISTMAS TOY FACTORY

#28 WEDDING CRASHER

#29 DOWN AND O DOWN UNDER

#30 THE MOUSE ISLAND MARATHON

#31 THE MYSTERIOUS CHEESE THIEF

CHRISTMAS CATASTROPHE

#32 VALLEY OF THE GIANT SKELETONS

#33 GERONIMO AND THE GOLD MEDAL MYSTERY

#34 GERONIMO STILTON, SECRET AGENT

#35 A VERY MERRY CHRISTMAS

#36 GERONIMO'S VALENTINE

#37 THE RACE ACROSS AMERICA

#38 A FABUMOUSE SCHOOL ADVENTURE

#39 SINGING SENSATION

#40 THE KARATE MOUSE

And don't forget to look for

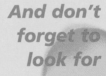

MIGHTY MOUNT KILIMANJARO

#42 THE PECULIAR PUMPKIN THIEF

THANKS FOR READING, AND GOOD-BYE UNTIL OUR NEXT ADVENTURE!

THEA SISTERS